Fergus and Marigold

For Chloe

First published in 1997 in Great Britain by
Piccadilly Press Ltd, London
www.piccadillypress.co.uk

Text and illustrations copyright © Tony Maddox 1997

This 2010 edition published by Sandy Creek by arrangement with Piccadilly Press

Sandy Creek
122 Fifth Avenue
New York, NY 10011

ISBN: 978 1 4351 2325 0

1 3 5 7 9 10 8 6 4 2

Printed and bound in China

Fergus and Marigold

Tony Maddox

Sandy Creek

Fergus wasn't happy.
He had been looking forward
to having a nice lazy day.
But Mrs. Coddle had brought
her cat Marigold to stay at the
farm for the day.
"Humph!" he thought grumpily.
"Cats are trouble!"

"I'll find somewhere quiet," thought Fergus, "where that cat won't bother me."

So he went to the big barn.

In the yard, Marigold was up to no good.
She jumped out at the hens
and gave them a scare.
"Cluck, Cluck, Cluck!" they squawked.

She crept up behind the ducks
and chased them into the duck pond.

"Quack, Quack, Quack!" they protested.

She even surprised the pigs
by pulling their curly tails.
"Oink, Oink, Oink!" they cried
angrily.

Clucking, quacking and oinking,
the animals rushed into the big barn
to hide from Marigold.
Fergus groaned.
"Some lazy day this is!" he thought.
"I'll have to find somewhere else to sleep."

When he looked out of the barn
he saw Marigold prowling around,
looking for more mischief.
"Woof, Woof!" he barked in warning.
The animals scrambled to find places
to hide.
"I'm off!" thought Fergus.

He hurried across the yard towards
the laundry hanging on the line.
A sudden gust of wind blew one of the
sheets which wrapped itself around him.

He yelped in surprise and
tried to get free.
Marigold turned to see
a scary white flapping thing
making the strangest yowling noise.
"Meeow!" she shrieked in fright.

She ran out of the yard, into
the orchard and up the nearest
apple tree.

When Fergus told the animals where Marigold was, they came to see for themselves.

She stayed up the apple tree until Farmer Bob climbed up his ladder and carried her down. "I think the animals must have scared her!" said Farmer Bob's wife.

"Humph!" said Fergus.